Dedication:

For my sweet Tessa and the crazy collection that started it all. - Jenna

For my gray bunny, who saw me through thick and thin for the first 8 years of my life, and for my parents; their generous donations and patience, to support my stuffed animal collection. - Mirka

Harmony Humbolt: The Perfect Pets Queen

Copyright 2021 by Jenna Grodzicki
Artwork Copyright 2021 by Mirka Hokkanen

Summary: Harmony Humbolt had a colossal collection of Perfect Pets. To everyone else, they might just be stuffed animals, but to Harmony they are EVERYTHING. Harmony hates leaving them home when she goes to school, so she figures out how to share them with her friends . . . with the right rules in place to keep them safe. When her list of rules continues to grow, her friends don't want to play with her perfect pets or her.

Can Harmony let go of her strict rules to enjoy both her perfect pets and her friends?

Clear Fork Publishing
P.O. Box 870 102 S. Swenson Stamford, Texas 79553 (325)773-5550
www.clearforkpublishing.com

Printed in the United States of America

ISBN - 978-1-950169-55-9
LCN -2021936733

HARMONY HUMBOLT

The Perfect Pets Queen

Written By

Jenna Grodzicki

Illustrated by

Mirka Hokkanen

Harmony Humbolt had a colossal collection of Perfect Pets. To most people, they were just stuffed animals. But to Harmony . . .

They meant everything.

Every morning, she counted them.
"One,
two,
three . . .
Ten!"

Every afternoon, she brushed their fur, straightened
their bows, and gave each one a snuggle.

And every night, she lined them up on her bed.

Going to
school meant
leaving her
Perfect Pets
behind.

That makes my stomach flutter, thought Harmony.

This didn't mean Harmony had to forget them, though.

She talked about them at lunch,

chatted about them during art,

and whispered about them during reading.

Her friends listened with wide eyes.

So, when she saw her teacher's note on the board, she felt like her wish had come true!

As Harmony placed her Perfect Pets in her backpack, her stomach began to flutter.

She wanted to share them, but they meant everything to her.

Harmony decided a plan was needed. Rules to keep her Perfect Pets safe.

Harmony's Rules:
1. Pick Your perfect Pet
2. Only 3. friends at a time.

When the recess bell rang, everyone gathered around Harmony. She shared her rules and handed out her Perfect Pets.

Thank you, Harmony!

AWESOME!

It's Perfect Pets paradise!

There were giggles and grins all around.

Until . . .
Harmony's stomach fluttered. "Is that jelly on your hands?"

Fiona started to lick it off, but
Harmony snatched up her Perfect Pets.

"Playtime's over," she
announced.

Harmony looked at her list.

Two rules are NOT enough.
She picked up her pencil.

New & Improvd

Harmony's ∧ Rules:

1. Pick your perfect Pet.

2 only 3 friends at a time.

3. No stikie fingrs.

At the next recess, Harmony chose three different friends to share her Perfect Pets and rules with.

Thanks for sharing your Perfect Pets!

Perfect Pets rule!

It's Perfect Pets' perfection!

Best of all, not a sticky finger was in sight.

Until . . .

Harmony's stomach fluttered. "Stop! You're squeezing the life out of Mr. Whiskers!"

Eddie shook his head, but Harmony swiped the Perfect Pets from everyone's hands.

Harmony looked at her list.
One more rule should do the trick.

The next day, recess was better than ever.
There were clean hands and gentle snuggles all around.
Just the way Harmony liked it.

Until . . .

Harmony's stomach fluttered. "Wait! Sir Woofington doesn't know how to fly!"

She plucked up
the Perfect Pets
one by one.

Harmony looked at her list.

Perfect Pets are NOT meant to fly.
Why didn't I think of this before?

Harmony's list grew

and grew.

But when it was time for recess . . .

No one wanted to
play with her or her
Perfect Pets.

Harmony sat alone on a bench.
All around her, friends were smiling
and laughing.
Harmony's stomach fluttered.
Her Perfect Pets meant
everything to her.

But . . . her friends did,
too.

That night, Harmony pulled out her list once more. She tore it into tiny pieces.

Then, she took out a fresh sheet of paper and began to write.

The next day, Harmony waved her friends over.
She held up her list.

Harmony's new rule was a hit! She snuggled, twisted, and twirled her Perfect Pets along with her friends.

They paraded the Perfect Pets
around the playground, with
Harmony leading the way.

She waited for her stomach to flutter but it never did.
Instead, sharing her Perfect Pets with happy friends made her feel like a queen . . .

A Perfect Pets Queen.

Eliana

Hooting, flapping, flying high, every nigh I'm in the sky.

The Perfect Pets Collection

Genevieve

Floppy ears and hopping feet, don't you think my dress is sweet?

The Perfect Pets Collection

Eliana

Hooting, flapping, flying high, every nigh I'm in the sky.

Fiona

Swimming, splashing near the ice, don't you think my tusks look nice?

Naomi

Rainbow mane and sparkling horn, that's where magic is born.

The Perfect Pets Collection

exp
In

Roxy

Bushy tail, and fur so red, pointy ears up on my head.

The Perfect Pets Collection

Mr Whiskers

Bowls of milk and balls of string, napping is my favorite thing.

The fect

Chewy

9 781950 169559